8,00 €

Heroes' Shrine for Sale

or

The Elegant Toilet

MARIOS HAKKAS

Heroes' Shrine for Sale
or
The Elegant Toilet

Translation
AMY MIMS

KEDROS

The translation costs of this book have been covered
by the Greek Ministry of Culture.

Acknowledgments

*With very special thanks for the valuable suggestions of Marika Hakka
and Maria Kyriazi-Peters.*

*Typeset in Greece
by Photokyttaro Ltd.
14, Armodiou St., Athens 105 52
Tel. 32.44.111
and printed by
M. Monteverdis & P. Alexopoulos
Metamorphosis, Athens
For
Kedros Publishers, S.A.,
3, G. Gennadiou St., Athens 106 78,
Tel. 38.09.712 – Fax 38.31.981
June 1997*

*Greek titles of the collections of short stories, various of which
are translated in this volume:* Ο μπιντές, Το κοινόβιο,
Ο τυφεκιοφόρος του εχθρού
Cover design by Dimitris Kalokyris

ISBN 960-04-1333-9

BY WAY OF A PROLOGUE
(Black and White)

OUT THERE, A WHITE ACROPOLIS, bright Parthenon, Erechtheion, Propylaea, all in marble.

"You're a little lap-dog. You bark, but the visitors are well aware you can't bite."

"You're a strange emancipator of canaries, which the cats will eat. You know they can't get along without a cage; freedom means lack of security. Why suffer and torture yourself?"

"You're a passenger on a boat rocking dangerously. Through your porthole, now you see the sky and then the sea. Intentionally, you confuse light and dark blue, dispensing with the horizon and joining the sky with the sea."

"You're an incureable 'ideocrat', with that tendency of yours to generalise, proceeding from the part to the whole. Without considering time and place, you end up with a few spectral ideas. With these you try to blackmail things, you bark, you open cages, but you cannot change things, because ultimately they determine your path, you are constantly stumbling against them, just as your curving course through the ship's corridor is from the rocking movement and its outermost limits are the walls of this corridor."

"It's about time you stop this grumbling. There's still some ground under your feet, solid ground for you to stand on and exist. Stop acting like an uprooted person. After all, history is what has actually happened and not what you wish would happen."

"I grant that – come what may – there is a space around me, some landscape, an engraving of autumn, an endless charred waste, rust-stained pine-trees laden with little sacks and caterpillars."

"I also grant that there's a path, bastinado-torture on the soles of the feet, permanent stone pressure under the heels, a path planted with stones which can break the toes."

"Here, my time has been spent on embellishing things. I've consumed my life in creating this landscape, in order to forge a human path. But I've ended up casting stones at the air."

"So many years in this futile war and I'm still struggling, barking even if I can't bite, writing angry slogans behind doors of public toilets, abandoned to the dangerous rocking of my own nerves, letting it trace my course, in the depths of winter opening cages of canaries, who'll be found like our dreams stiff in the gutter or like wings travelling up above the courtyards, streets and rooftops – downy feathers."

"Out there now, a grey Acropolis is clearly outlined, an ashen Parthenon, a dry slate-wall Erechtheion, cement-colured Propylaea, and the Temple of Wingless Victory a common dirt grave for our own broken wings ..."

THE FRESCO OF KESARIANI

IN THE MONASTERY OF KESARIANI, there is a fresco in three phases: "the man that fell among the thieves", exactly like the well-known description in the Bible. A traveller is caught by some thieves: there's a round of "trouncing"; then the stalwart bullies depart, lined up like an army, with their cudgels on their shoulders; then a passerby picks up the man who's been thrashed.

At first glance, we observe the poor workmanship in this fresco. Maybe this creates a new aesthetic outlook, like everything initially in bad taste; but needless to say, I'm not interested from this point of view. I care that this allegedly poor workmanship causes a different meaning from that of the original parable and this suits certain events, which took place in the neighbourhood of Kesariani.

It's that uniformity of the faces – traveller-thieves-passerby – the very same faces. I'm not talking about the uncovered parts of the body (besides, these are minimal) and the garments with their folds (all of them identical), as though the fresco-painter had only one model. I mean the faces, the faces of "the man that fell" and the man who didn't fall are all the same. If a single twitch had been added to the faces of the thieves as they raise their cudgels to beat up the fallen traveller; or if an expression of pain had been painted on the latter's face, the similarity between the fresco and present-day Kesariani would have been spoiled.

The basic conclusion is that the same person thrashes, is thrashed and tends to the healing.

Now I understand why Honis (alias "Mama's Bun"), who used to shout Resistance catchwords through the loudhailer, became a Fascist later on and beat up the others, who were now shouting the same catchwords (even though they used to beat up "Mama's Bun" for shouting them). Same persons, same faces: identical model.

This also explains a bloke nicknamed "Rouhou-Mouhou", who used to steal clothes from the laundry-line and act as a police informer. When he left Officer Davilas' house, where he'd delivered his information, he pinched the washing from the clothes-line; they caught him and he got a sound drubbing, but he still went on taking information to Davilas; except now, when he left the house, he didn't find any clothes to snatch, because Davilas' wife had taken the precaution to hide them.

"We're all in the same boat, stewing in our own juice," in the words of an old man from Kesariani. Observing the fresco, I quite agree – except for the dead. They are outside the game, any kind of game. But I don't know how long this stewing will continue

and what sort of broth it'll offer in the end. I'm afraid
it may already have offered everything it was supposed to; either because the pan is full of holes or
because the stewing has stopped. Human beings burn
out; new circumstances bypass the previous set-up –
radio, television, electricity and telephone bills. Nick-
names are gradually disappearing. Blocks of flats are
mushrooming up along the boulevard and there are
tar-paved roads surrounding the lanes.

I suspect this meaning of the fresco is at an end
and another more up-to-date meaning is about to be
expressed: this lax uniformity of the consumer society; something general, which is spreading like a
monster throughout all Athens.

Kesariani, with your grocer's i.o.u.–chits and your
peddler selling lice-repellent for the hair, you are dead
now. Kesariani, with that coprophagic Moukoutsou (I
saw him leaning against the wall of the outdoor gym,
eating his own excrement, by way of a bet for a bit of
worthless Occupation money); subsequently, he
became a squealer and terrorising bully for both fac-
tions. Primitive Kesariani, you no longer exist.

Nevertheless, my own mind and my love are for
Kesariani of the "trouncing" era and I feel lucky to
have grown up there. Everything was wild and vir-
ginal, in its first genesis, as in ancient tragedy: Jason,
the first walking tree, leaps into the sea and sets sail
for Colchis. Oedipus, all tangled up at the borderline,
goes blind in the first light of an explosive thermal
flash. And Creon appears for the first time in history,
holding a bunch of keys. All things are at the source,

in their original state of revelation, which is why people, neighbourhoods and events refuse to fade inside me.

A place inhabited for the first time. A long narrow uphill strip with scanty wild shrubs. To the left, the riverbed and a forest of skinny, sickly pine-trees. To the right, the walled enclosure of the Skopeftirion Grove. High up, the Monastery. Tent, shack, mud-brick hut and patchwork rug of the refugees – there you are, Kesariani, smiling in the first sun.

Kesariani of the public urinals; Kesariani of the milkman spreading propaganda for Russia till the refugees from Vourla* got hold of him with their big sticks. Kesariani of the donkey-heads people had to eat in the Occupation, and the entrails stuffed with blood and spices, and the "balls" made of wild asphodels, I thank you for letting me grow up in your narrow lanes. What could anyone who'd ever lived in Messolonghi divulge? He'd be weighed down by the past and the myth. For him, everything was over by the time he got close; even the deterioration of the place was completed before him.

Kesariani, thank you for giving me the chance to see and touch a few people, who got away in time, before they could be listed in any meaning of the fresco, either the trouncers or the consumers. Lefteris, Missus Evdokia's brother – "Aslan-Lefteris, Kaplan-Lefteris" – who was executed in Corfu later

* Name of Greek town, in Asia Minor, from which various refugees moved to Kesariani.

on. Poutsouris, my playmate with wooden swords and paper caps, until he held a real rifle in his hands – the lad was fifteen years old, when a bullet shot him in the forehead near the Poseidon *kafeneion*. Thank you for allowing me to see Apollo's blue jacket, the bluest blue in my whole life, made of pure sky and sea. And Aris, who was killed at the corner of Damareos Street and Formionos, and on that very spot, I saw the corpses of several collaborators, with their identity-card hidden in their socks. Righteous, swift retribution, an automatic catharsis for the place.

Kesariani, who shall I remind you of first? Ignatios, who died for nothing. He was the neighbourhood idiot and he'd been misled by the general climate. He stuck a wooden shoe in his back pocket, pretended it was a pistol, and made the rounds of the various districts, always on the alert. One day they caught him in this suspicious position and they shot him and he was done for too.

Kesariani, once you were a star; for a moment, you shone bright in the firmament and then, you vanished for ever into the void of history.

Now, you old slut, you eat sirupy semolina-sweets and fluted honey-cakes; you munch your roasted gourd-seeds in the outdoor summer cinema and spit the little shells at the necks of respectable shop-owners, wholesale grocers, butchers, contractors, who want to rid themselves of your shame. From one standpoint, I agree with the Mayor for wanting to change your name. How can you be connected with these petty persons, the spirit of private property and

apartment-building deals? They'll call you Nea Vri-
oula or Neo Syvissarion.* It's better. What else
remains from the Saint Antoine quarter of Paris,
except its name? In the form of songs, your parallel
steppes have been irrigated; Canton is under con-
struction; Kokkinia** has been altered to Nikaia; the
worthiest of your children have been lopped off.
That's how it always is after a savage timber-felling
and the few remaining trees are rotten. Let me not
take a roll-call now "of the living and the dead"...
"world without end". End of the season and the sales
about to follow.

Kesariani, I am sweating. Kesariani, I'm choking.
Kesariani, I retch. You sit there in the twilight, enjoy-
ing the cool air on your sidewalks, while your young
girls, clutching their little handbags, stroll down
towards the public square. You drink your almond-
juice with the money you earn as a broker and you
belch. In your expression, I can sense repentance; you
seem to be sorry for not being by birth a go-between,
a scheming bitch and collaborator.

Where is your valour and where is your freedom,
my gazelle and doe and hind? Where is your beauty
and where are your jewels, you frigate and schooner
and corvette?

There's nothing left. Now you're plastering the last
traces of gunshots on your brow, like an old dog lick-

---

* Names of other Asia Minor towns, homelands of other
Kesariani refugees.
** The name of a militant left-wing district of Athens.

ing its wounds where the scar has healed. Now you are downtrodden, broken, exhausted, in the final phase of the fresco, trying to heal and forget the fierce events of your journey.

THE HOLY WATER OF KESARIANI

IN KESARIANI UP AT THE MONASTERY, there's a spring. The water flows out of the mouth of a ram, an ancient pagan invention, and all the women who drank water from the ram gave birth to children and male children, at that. This is how the myth goes, an original kind of mating, tupping with water. With water? Yes indeed, when it comes from the mouth of an animal, which is capable of visiting whole flocks of ewes, anything is possible. A lovely, quite paganistic conception and extremely realistic.

In Byzantine times, when things became more spiritualised, some monk, or maybe Time as well (I don't quite know) cut the ram's horns slightly, so it would look rather like a lamb. This wasn't very successful, because despite its truncated horns, the ram still insists on looking like a ram. However, of necessity, the water lost its former attributes and became holy water, "for all manner of sickness and all manner of disease".

In our own day, the ram-lamb is just a decoration and nothing more, and the water is merely good mineral water for the digestion. That's how myths come

to an end and science arrives to explain some inexplic-
able phenomena; dialectic arrives and examines the
interacting influence of water and revolutionary psy-
chology. That's the way I am too: armed to the teeth
with dialectic, I intend to interpret the behaviour of
the people of Kesariani throughout these past thirty
years, exclusively in terms of this water, as my guide.

An hour's trek from the last houses in the district
is no small matter. You arrive perspiring and
exhausted from that upward climb and you pitch into
the water, which (as we said) has a specific attribute.
It rinses out your vitals. Is the water to blame if
you're hungry? Is it to blame if you don't have anything to eat? From up here, with a panorama of the
city spread out in front of you, you become revolutionary and you rush forth. This is the case of Kesariani
throughout the Occupation.

The woodcutters dug to find arbutus roots. Other
people scavenged for turtles. The women picked the
last of the wild greens. Nothing was left on the mountain. Only nettles for stew and this water, but as soon
as you drank it, it turned your intestines into a flute.
The jackknives they'd used to pick the greens grew
rusty, the pickaxes idle and their faces were all
sunken. That's how heroes are born, donkeys' heads,
and "balls" made out of wild asphodel-greens. Everything's a matter of necessity. That's how countries
become great and then, some pen-pushers who fabricate myths appear and tell you about intangible ideas,
maidens and goddesses who descend from the mountains. That means nothing. They are brought by the

stomach and taken away by the stomach, ideas are fairies with faces like round round loaves of bread, with black black eyes like olives, with peaches for cheeks and breasts filled with milk or rice. You go on the rampage when you lack all these things (call it an idea, call it Freedom, it's all the same to me). You grab hold of the flag and dash out into the streets, yearning for a good round of gunfire. Anyhow, the cold breath of hunger is creeping up from behind.

What's come over me, why do I keep ridiculing everything? Perhaps things are actually serious and the ridiculous lodges inside me. In any case, since I've set my goal as the debunking of certain situations, it's out of the question for me to fabricate other myths. It's better to express ridicule. If I'd seen things this way from the start, maybe I'd have escaped the fanfares and pointless hurrahs and big words, and that phrase *"our* Kesariani". Why *"our"* and not *"their"*? What the devil sort of private property contract have we signed and – although we're sunk in clouds of pompous phrases – why must Kesariani belong to us, at all costs?

But for once, let's try to talk in a serious tone: Freedom, we are browsing like lambs, we are bleating for the milk of your breasts. Freedom, we await you as we wait for some heaven-sent gift; in books we plead for you. Freedom, I have written you upon the mountain as well as on the sea; I've made my lungs bleed for you and I've wasted my youth. Freedom... out of the way, cut the melodrama. Kick it away, give it a smack, let's end this fabricating of myth.

Freedom of the courtyard, ouzo and backgammon in company with my brother-in-law, it's you I cherish. Freedom of the weekly job and the Sunday excursion, it's you I adore. Freedom, with a small plot of land and a savings account book, I bought you off. Freedom, my motor-car races on at a hundred-twenty kilometres per hour, a grand speed, I don't have time to glance even at the trees, how could I possibly see the hands and the chains? Freedom, how do you like my new necktie and my shirt with the trendy collar? What suit shall I wear, when (and if) you come? And what about the boot department? Nice, eh, to boot? Wherever I walk, there's a creaking sound – needless to say, it's not from the earth. I used to walk barefoot and the earth did creak. Another era. Freedom, now I'm on a diet, since I know you always crown slim men with success. Age has taken us in tow, potbelly, (I wonder if this bulging thing is from my necktie?), clear signs of going bald, what can we do? I drink my whiskey and try to forget you. If my shoe pinches me tomorrow, maybe I'll think about you a bit.

From the last houses of Kesariani, it's hardly ten minutes by car up to the monastery. You jump out, fresh as a daisy, clutching a big basket and a plastic jug and you head for the plane-trees. From a distance, the ram is observing you: "I say, what's come over this fellow?" the ram wonders. "Why doesn't he come any closer?" "Let me get some food in my belly," you gesture to the ram. You open your basket and start off with the *tzatziki*-salad and octopus as appetizers. "I'm coming," you tell the ram, as you pop over to the spring and arrange the first course. Then back to the basket and the jug of wine; and out come the fried meat-balls and out come the titbits of liver and out comes the chicken – the second course. "You bitchy deep freeze (say you), what're you doing to me? You've overthrown Marxism." Now you sit down under the plane-trees and the ram goes on observing you so very aloofly. "How far can he go?" says the ram. "He'll have to come back and then, we'll butt horns." You are holding your belly (swollen now like an oblong watermelon) and straining at every muscle, you rise to your feet. Fine! Luckily there's that mineral water. "Shall we open a tin of Russian crabs?" you ask your comrade. "You bitch, preserved goods, you've shattered Leninism as well. That's finished too. There's nothing left standing. As for ideas, with such a full stomach, how can I think. Maybe tomorrow." (Post-Occupation status of Kesariani.)

THE GOLDFISH IN THE GLASS BOWL

THE MAN WITH THE LOAF OF BREAD under his arm is the same person who approximately two years ago, was holding a watermelon. Then, it had been July and naturally, there were watermelons, whereas now it was April and he'd bought a loaf of bread. Of course, even if there were watermelons (which is quite unnatural for the month of April), he'd still go to the bakery for a loaf of bread, just like everyone else.

In the general panic, everybody pounced on the food supplies. He too waited his turn about half-an-hour and in the end, found himself holding a steaming hot loaf. Other people were buying three or four loaves, but he got only one. The business he wanted it for required only one. He put it under his armpit and started to roam the streets.

When somebody's holding a loaf of bread, the correct thing is to go home. But our man couldn't go. In the neighbourhood where he lived, they'd begun arresting people at the crack of dawn and he'd barely had time to hurry into his clothes; then he'd rushed out in search of the most suitable object to camouflage his movements.

All people, even primitive people, know about the use-value of objects. In advanced commercial countries, of course things also have another value: the exchange-value, as it's usually called. In Greece, in addition to these two well-known values, which are in great demand, a third value has also been discovered: the "interchange-value", which plays such a role in the extraordinary circumstances this country so often lives through. The "interchange-value" of a thing is directly proportionate to the inventiveness of the "interchanger" (masquerader) and the intelligence of the police officer he is trying to deceive. In a word, the cleverer the policeman is, the more convincing the object which the "interchanger" (masquerader) is holding must be – in order for the "interchange-law" to function.

During the July events,* when our man went to the rallies (as a matter of fact, always on the outer fringe), he used to hold a watermelon. ("Interchange-value.") If there was any trouble, he used to slip away, pointing to the watermelon when he met a policemen. "I'm a law-abiding citizen and I'm just on my way home."

In actual fact, he did go home, put on his pyjamas and slippers, and sitting there on his verandah, he cut the watermelon and ate it (now, it's the use-value), till the rinds were like papyrus. This was his evening

---

* The violent demonstrations of July 1965, which led to the April 21st, 1967 coup of the Colonels – this particular April late afternoon, commemorated in the present story.

meal. In recent years he'd been gorging himself on whatever came his way and he'd grown very heavy on sauces, so he decided to make a diet. But his belly still stuck out there in front of him like an oblong watermelon, and though he kept saying he would start exercising the next day, this never happened. He was bored. Too bored even to deal with the wrought-iron objects which decorated his verandah, because they needed a coat of white paint. There was also the goldfish in the glass bowl and every so often, he was supposed to change the water; but this was also an occupation he found boring.

In recent years, he too had his Capua-retreat. A little house with a verandah facing the mountain. After spending half his life in prison wards and tents on exile-islands, after all those deprivations, one day when he found himself free, he got involved in some land speculation, suddenly earned a bit of money and he'd bought this little house, where he lived all on his own.

He couldn't make up his mind to get married. "You never know what may happen," he said each time that topic of conversation was brought up. "Marriage ties you down to this world, responsibilities, children. I'm a man with a past and an uncertain future."

However, even without marriage – only with the house – he was tightly tied down to this world and there was an unbridgeable gap from his past. It wasn't only because of the framed pictures decorating the four walls and windows free of iron bars and a door he could open whenever he pleased – of course,

these weren't enough reasons for him to break with
his previous life. There was also the Danish style furniture for his living-room. There was also a bed with
a comfortable stromatex mattress. A stove for the
winter nights, a fridge for the torrid summers, ice-
cubes and a heap of other little items which at first
glance, he'd never encountered during those heroic,
but really hard years of his youth.

It's true, he hadn't made a total break with his
past. As much as he could, he carried on, by attending
the rallies (according to party-orders, of course), by
sending in his subscription regularly, and by listening
to his gramophone play records which referred exclusively to those difficult years.

It was nice to hear these records describing sor-
rows and deprivations, that superhuman endeavour
(regardless of whether it didn't end up anywhere) and
that heroic attitude he himself had shared. It was
very nice indeed to sit on your chaise-longue and day-
dream, even about things which had pained you in
the past, but were smoother now. They were all
wreathed in myth now, as though they had never happened to you. "Eh, that's all over. Difficult years, but
there was a sort of beauty about this story." It was
really nice at home with his memories and his record-
player; it was very nice indeed the way he lived; damn
it all, why had they started up again? What was
wrong and he'd be forced to roam the streets again?

He was sitting pretty and now the witch-hunt had
begun and where could he go? Which wary door could
he knock on, since everybody – relatives, acquain-

tances, friends – would be in the same boat? Many of them would already have been arrested by now and others like himself would perhaps be wandering around holding a loaf of bread.

He made a big detour far from the city-centre. After passing through the neighbourhoods of Vironas and Dafni, he landed in Kallithea. It was good exercise. For some time now, he hadn't done this much walking. And it was a bright morning, which seemed made expressly for a long walk, Absent-mindedly he began nibbling a corner of the loaf, and at the same moment, optimistic thoughts came to him: "I say, this situation can't last long. Soon enough, they'll collapse."

Now anyone who wishes to examine this dictum more closely might observe that the vagueness of the first sentence continues into the second sentence and this is due to the use of the third person. Of course, the use of the first person (and indeed, in the singular, in this specific case) calls for valour and personal coaching for such a contingency. "How will they collapse?" he could hear a voice inside him asking. "Like ripe fruits, of their own accord? Or by giving the tree a really hard shake?" "They'll be overthrown by the People," he corrected himself, with a slightly bitter taste, because it was taken for granted that he considered himself one with the People and consequently, could not run away from the trouble. Yes, but in that case, he should get a move on, he should go to the city-centre where incidents might take place, he should participate in them. Or did he perhaps believe in the theory of the vanguard (party-members are needed) and therefore he should take cover?

"I can't," he said to himself. "My feet just won't take me as far as the centre. Though I see it's the right thing to do, it's impossible for me. Let the others take action; the young people can go down to the city-centre."

He'd reached a neighbourhood, where a distant cousin of his lived. He was reluctant to visit her home. But his mouth was bitter with cigarettes and he needed some coffee. In the end, he made up his mind.

"What's up?" his cousin's husband asked; he was a hefty bloke with a hefty salary.

"What's up?" he asked back, not knowing what to answer.

"Will there be a football-match on Sunday, eh?"

"How should I know?" he answered, coming from outside.

"What a muck-up! What a muck-up! On the radio, they're broadcasting only marches. Not a word about football."

Our man slurped his coffee, though it was scalding-hot, and tried to escape from his cousin's husband and the heavy music on the radio as fast as possible; he rushed out into the street again, this time at a nervous, spry pace. It was the first time he walked like this and he was puzzled when he caught himself concentrating on a military march, almost actually humming it:

"Our Great Artillery,
our Great Artillery
Our Great Artillery
will save our brave country!"

He observed that another man in front of him was walking in the same rhythm, at the same pace, as though there were some microscopic loudspeakers glued to his ears and broadcasting the same familiar march. He was lugging a bag stuffed with supplies of food and this made him lose the beat each time. But right away, with a little hop, he found the beat again. Our man trailed after him. Two blocks further up, the latter vanished behind a door. Maybe a wife in a nightgown was expecting him, or the neighbours across the way for a jigger of ouzo, or his brother-in-law with the backgammon-board all lined up. For him, nothing changed. With just one little hop, right away, he was in rhythm with the day and this permitted him to sleep in his own home.

So why shouldn't he make this little compromise? Why should he always walk out-of-step? Acceptance of the situation is a trifle and afterwards, you can go back home. Needless to say, there might not be a wife in a nightgown expecting him, or a brother-in-law or neighbours to keep him company; but he did have that little goldfish in the glass bowl and who would change its water? It was a living creature too, a real responsibility. He imagined it swimming about in the cramped space of the glass bowl. With graceful movements, it was displaying its golden belly, then its side fins. Its mouth kept opening and closing rhythmically. But all of a sudden, it started breathing very fast; it was suffocating. Now it was wriggling, it was drowning, its body was sinking leaden down to the bottom of the glass bowl.

He took his handkerchief out of his back pocket and wiped his perspiring brow. "Impossible," he thought to himself. "I *must* go." He must take care of that little fish. The only thing he could do on this crucial day was to change the water for the goldfish. He didn't have the strength for those other serious and great matters.

On this April late afternoon, he was going back home and his decision was made. He would lock himself in and they could come by his house to get him. With dusk falling, he was back in Kesariani.

YANNIS, THE GIANT ANT

THEY DRAGGED HIM CUMBERSOMELY into the detention-cell. Three a.m., his bellowing roars woke me up, rousing the entire station as well. My heavenly dream was abruptly interrupted. I just had time to slip on my trousers. The hubbub out in the corridor indicated they were carting him in, but a cart with frequent stops, as though it were climbing uphill laden with iron.

"Damn it all, do we have to deal with you now?" I could hear the police guard's voice and at the same moment, a thud like a fist pounding on a cement column. Then, the officer on duty, who was gentler: "Come on, Yannis, let's get it over with."

The door opened and Yannis filled all the space. A colossus tall as the rafters blocked the door, got stuck there and refused to budge another inch. In back of him, the huffing and puffing of the guard and the officer could be heard, as they struggled to shove him in there, as though into a closet stuffed with books.

"Come on now, Yannis, get it over with. We've got other things to do."

"I'm not going in there. I'm not a commie!" I could make out through his confused words, the roar of a lion. I held on to the corner of the bed, livid with fear, and I waited.

"Till you sober up," the other person insisted, still pushing.

"I knock the daylights out of the commies!" and he tried to clench his fists, though he was still holding on to the frame of the door, two sledgehammer fists, shaking them in front of his blurry eyes. A well-coordinated push from the other two men finally got him in there, and the door closed behind him, was hastily bolted, and the footsteps of the two "porters" retreated.

At first, he tended to his wrinkled jacket, particularly the two lapels which had fallen. His attitude was a mixture of anger and bewilderment; he seemed to feel terribly degraded, a kind of unfrocking, as though his epaulets had been ripped off, or something like that. Then he banged his fist against the wall in despair, roaring drunken remarks, which ended up with the familiar refrain:

"I knock the daylights out of the commies!"

Cringing in my corner, I didn't let out a sound. A stinging April wind was blowing through the screen and iron frame of the window, causing a chilly draft from the peep-hole in the door. My terror-stricken eyes flickered quickly back and forth between Yannis and the door. So far, he acted as though he hadn't even noticed me.

"This honoured khaki," he said to me now, turning round and pointing to his torn army shirt.

I nodded by way of acquiescence, moved very gently towards the peep-hole and called out as steadily as I could:

"Officer!"

"What is it?" came a voice from the back.

"Come here a minute."

"What's up?"

I stuck my snout into the peep-hole and whispered: "What about him?"

"He'll sober up. In the morning, we'll let him go."

"You're responsible for my life. You can hear the mood he's in."

The officer on duty shrugged his shoulders, indifferently.

"We don't have another detention-cell."

How would the night end? I'd spent ten lazy, relaxed days here, ten days with sporadic visits from freshly-arrested political prisoners, who were bundled off as soon as they received blankets from home and went straight to the Transit Station–boat–exile island. I was left in a sweet state of solitude, with extremely polite police guards, no interrogation, plenty of food, milk, sleep, reading, dreams, thoughts.

And all of a sudden, here I was, in the lion's den, beteen two hands as big as spades; by the time I could manage to call out and let the officer know what was happening in the cell, Yannis – a lawless state machine wild as a wine-press out-of-control – would have crushed me.

He stood up and staggered to the door.

"Officer," he roared. Not a sound. "Guard, guard," he hollered again and again, shaking the door. No answer. His hands, which had been gripping the iron bars, hung loose, gradually relaxed, dangling like broken wings.

He was feeling somewhat better; then he turned around with a sly manner and said to me:

"For you, they come. For me, nothing doing."

I looked at him severely, keeping him at a certain distance.

"I understand," he said. "You're one of those blokes they stick in here in order to fish us. What a nice trick. But I'm right wing!"

How did I think of that casual answer:

"We'll see about that."

"You'll see, you'll see. Here in the 19th Security Station, everybody knows me. I don't bother anyone. In the morning, when the boys come, they all know me. You must be new, eh?" and with a grimace, he tried to smile.

"Here, it's the Tenth Station," I told him abruptly. "Pangrati."

"Pangrati? Tenth Station?" he was puzzled and looked around, anxiously. He seemed reassured, but his swollen lips were quivering: "What happens now? What the hell was I doing in Pangrati?" he reproached himself. "What do we do now, mister?" he appealed to me ever so politely.

"We'll ask the Security Police down below," I answered him, with a self-assured air, stepping directly into the role. "We'll have a look at your file."

He skulked off into the corner, hanging his head and muttering through his teeth:

"I'm extreme right!"

"Pipe down now. Come on, sleep."

"Fine, fine, mister.

"Stop roaring."

"Fine, fine, mister."

"I hope you don't snore?"

"Fine, fine, mister. But I'm right wing and I do snore."

"Aha! We won't get along then. Cut out the snoring."

I tossed off my blanket and stood up on the bed in a threatening pose. He collapsed on his knees, folded his hands entreatingly, twisted his fingers together, beseeching in such a foolish way he provoked me.

"I'll try, Officer. The file doesn't mean anything. Back in those days, we all were. Even our cats were. In the Occupation we were hungry. All of us went. I used a rifle too. But afterwards, I gave it back."

"But afterwards? Afterwards, why did you go back again?"

"Afterwards? Afterwards?" with a lost expression, he stared at the peep-hole, laughing an imbecilic little laugh, seeking the answer on the empty walls, the ceiling, even glancing under the bed.

"Afterwards?" I asked again.

"Afterwards – because I'd been there before," he accepted his condemnation in a disgruntled way.

"What did you do?"

"No rifles. Slogans on the walls. I've told all this to the 19th Security Station. I was a house-painter and I knew how to mix colours. That's why."

"Red colours, eh?"

He seemed not to have heard; he changed the subject and his face lit up.

"Afterwards, this honoured khaki."

"But on Makronissos."*

"Yes," once more he'd found his terrified mask.

"You recanted."

"Yes, indeed."

"Afterwards, you still refused to cool it. You used to go to the demonstrations. And down to headquarters."

A wild animal caught in a trap, no longer making any effort to escape. An ant whose antennae had been cut off. He was innocuous. He was no longer drunk. Through the window, the first semi-white light of dawn was trickling in. The light-bulb up above was turning ochre-coloured. I felt sleepy. I missed the sweet solitude of the detention-cell all to myself.

"All right, you'll get out."

I went to the peep-hole and called:

"Officer!"

"What's up?"

"Yannis is o.k."

"Good. I'll be right there."

Yannis' face reflected the idiotic thankfulness of common people towards a benefactor. He shook my hand heartily.

---

* The most dreaded of the detention-islands for political prisoners, especially during and after the Greek Civil War (1947-1949).

"Thanks. Come and meet me some night for a bit of wine at Kollimenos' taverna."

"No big deal," I answered listlessly.

"At my expense. Please tell me your name."

"I'm Yannis too."

"So we've got the same name," he was pleased.

Out in the corridor, footsteps were heard. They unlocked the door and it opened.

"Goodbye," he called to me.

The officer on duty and two plain-clothes men came in.

"So that's how it is, Mr. Yannis!" said the officer. "You've filled Pangrati with slogans. We've arrested the other bloke and he's testified to everything."

The two plain-clothes men began searching him. They turned his trouser-pockets inside out. There were bright red paint-stains on them.

"What have you done with the paint-brush? Fine, we'll send you down below and there, you'll tell us everything."

"You there," the officer on duty ordered me, "get your things and get out."

That night, I went to the taverna. He wasn't there. After some time, I went back again. He was still missing. I asked about Yannis. He was still in jail.

THE PRISONER
WITH THE THUNDERING SNORE

HE ENTERED THE WARD WITH HIS suitcases bulging half-open from the search. The guard's hands had excavated deep down and brought to light some household commodities too rich for a convicted man. Brand-new clothes, modern shoes, elegantly bound books. On top of the open English cot, beautiful warm blankets had been unfolded and three shopping-nets chock-full of food supplies.

He started by handing out cigarettes to the men surrounding him. The first pack finished and he brought out another pack.

"Take some, mate," he kept saying, as he offered the large-size, de luxe pack.

"What prison did you come from?" someone asked.

"From Yannina," the new man answered.

"Did you stay there some time?"

"About a month."

"Only a month and they transferred you?" the other man was puzzled.

He didn't answer and continued handing out the pack towards the outer ring of the constantly growing circle. Polite fingers hastily caressed the interior of

the packet, which was drained with lightning speed
and replaced by another full pack.

"On my way through Athens, my brothers came to
visit me at the Transit Station. They loaded me down
with heaps. I've got more in the suitcase. Take some
more, mate."

"Let the man arrange his things and then, you can
talk with him. Excuse me, my friend, what's your
name?"

"Moutafis."

"Excuse me. I'm the warden and I'm concerned
about keeping order in here."

"Can't you distribute this food," asked Moustafis,
"to one and all?"

"All the food?"

"Of course, all of it. I've also got a one-thousand-
drachma note. Keep nine-hundred."

"That's not correct," said the warden. "You should
give me only fifty percent."

"Poppycock," answered Moustafis. "I don't need it.
Just enough for some cigarettes."

The warden was right. Only fifty percent of individual income belonged to the group of political prisoners co-existing there. This was an inviolable principle for whatever concerned money and food. Half of
whatever came by cheques, visits, packages, belonged
to the whole group. Rather similar to the Christian
parable of the two coats. Although in reality, the
prison principle was somewhat inferior, of course,
because the tunics, greatcoats, army-boots, clothing
in general, were an exception; they weren't part of

the social game, they were absolutely a matter of individual property, so that a blend of the two systems resulted – something like a transitional N.E.P., combining prison needs for the whole group and individual needs.

However, nobody could prevent Moutafis from violating this rule, these principles (needless to say, in an upwards direction). No one could stop him from behaving for the benefit of the whole, ignoring his own personal needs.

So after getting rid of the food (spread like superfluous trash all over his cot) and also the thousand-drachma note, (threatening to burn a hole in his pocket), he handed his two new room-mates (the ones exactly next to him) two of his three brand-new starched shirts and three of his five blankets.

Perhaps in this way he felt as though he were doubling his quota, with the joy of "overbalancing" his "plan", the inner rejoicing of the man who has tamed his own flesh. In the eyes of his comrades in the ward, he appeared to be a perfect human being, a person who'd made good and was doing his duty towards his neighbour – literally his neighbours, two fellow-prisoners whose paraphernalia lay just to his left and his right. To be sure, the distribution wasn't absolutely fair. One could observe that he distributed his belongings inversely, according to the distance from where he himself was placed. The prisoners closest to his cot got the most and the ones furthest away got least. The one sleeping over there in the corner of the ward received only a simple undershirt. Anyway, what matters is that by evening, when the bell rang for bed-time, Moutafis was left with empty suitcases.

He spread out his two remaining blankets as nicely as possible and then, he settled down to listen to the breathing of his comrades, as they fell asleep one by one with their eyelids tightly closed; he could hear the extreme serenity prevailing in the ward, the calm night tiptoeing in order not to alarm all these bodies which had surrendered themselves. It seemed to him he could see their dreams gliding through the iron bars, ambling noiselessly out in the yard, climbing the pine-tree and the tiled rooftop of the prison, to gaze out beyond.

His affectionate gaze fell on the cots, embracing the twenty prisoners, who'd surrendered to their first sleep.

"Without these men, I can't live," he reflected. "Without them. I'll go to pieces. I can't stand being on my own any more. They must understand. I can't get along without the group. At some point, I'll be unable to bear the tyranny of the night. I'm a political prisoner and my place is here with them. I can't live all by myself in disciplinary guard-rooms, alone with my own thoughts, far from the group, far from my own people, at night when the prison closes."

By now, the fatigue of the day, the journey trans-ferring him, the new acquaintances, started pressing down on his eyelids, numbing his limbs. He realised that sleep was closing in on him.

"Sleep-death," he reflected yet again. He tried to chase it away. "No, no, not yet. I must avoid it. If only I could throw a bit of water on my eyes. If only I weren't so tired from the trip, maybe I could escape. Maybe for one more evening, I'd be able to live the warmth of the ward, the recognition of these human beings, my comrades, whom I love so very much."

He could no longer resist. He felt it coming from deep down like wind, then a shapeless mass, with a spider's movements. "It's coming," he reflected and he sank. Now it was creeping on the floor, sneakily like a squid. All of a sudden, an enormous monster lunged at him and grabbed hold of him. He felt totally paralysed. First, it stuck to his arms. Then it wound itself around his legs like a chain of barbecued *koko-retsi*-meat. Then it landed on his eyes. Darkness. He was suffocating. He opened his mouth to catch his breath, a deep breath, and the monster wormed its way inside. With methodical movements, it spread its limbs towards his pharynx, his nostrils, his larynx, everywhere filling his mouth with its thick gooey body. He tried to vomit it up, with a deep breath out-wards he tried to cast it out far away. He tried again and again. But it stuck there even more. Spreading its tentacles down deeper towards his stomach, his lungs, till it reached his heart and from there crept on to his arteries. He tried to scream "Help" and make a move, in hopes that a still deeper exhalation might dislodge it. An even deeper breath. Now it had reached his brain; from there, it rushed on to his spine; it had started to paralyse him. One more breath out. He was drowning. Breathe in-breathe out; breathe in-breathe

out. Let him get free of it, let him not suffocate.
Breathe in...

"Wake him up," the warden ordered in a soft tone,
but his voice was lost in the pandemonium which had
been jarring the ward for quite a while now.

This wasn't a snore. It had started out as a small
roar, then the distant thundering of an imminent
storm. Then big boulders landsliding onto a heap of
rocky debris, knocking against each other, dragging
down other boulders, constantly landsliding down
into a deep ravine, detaching cornerstones which
shattered on the rocks, a ravine whose very foundations were shaking, as all the stones in the whole wide
world were falling simultaneously, unhindered, without stopping anywhere, even for a rest, – this roar
kept increasing, from one heap of debris to the next,
from ravine to ravine, from gorge to gorge, never-ending gullies leading to other gullies...

"Wake him up," someone yelled fiercely.

The entire ward was sitting up on the cots. With a
wrathful eye, they were all staring towards the side of
the ward where that never-stopping roar was coming
from.

"Hey there Yannis, prod him."

"I've prodded him three times already. He just
won't wake up," said the man next to Moutafis.

"Give him a harder shake. We won't get a wink of
sleep all night."

"Wake him up, the bugger," howled the man in the
corner, who'd received only the undershirt.

"Hey man, wake him up. What're you waiting for?

You wanna alarm the whole prison?" the guard's voice was heard saying behind the peep-hole.

From the neighbouring wards, they were banging on the wall. In all the wards, rudely awakened heads appeared near the windows, wondering what was going on.

"Make the bastard stand up," the man in the corner shouted again. "Give him a few slaps and he'll wake up."

"So that's why he was transferred from Yannina in a month's time."

"Hey, what a windfall for us!" another man said.

The warden had rushed in by now and was shaking Moutafis; after forcing him to his feet, he yelled:

"Wake up!... Wake up!... Wake up!..."

With dazed eyes, Moutafis gaped at this furious throng gesticulating in his direction, shouting in loud voices, some of the men barefooted on the cement floor, holding their underpants, others standing on their cots, staring glumly in his direction.

"Forgive me, lads," he managed to stammer. "It's an incureable disease. Tomorrow, I'll report for morning-call and ask to be transferred again."

BOUBOUKA

THE PRISON WAS JUST CLOSING. Behind the stone wall, the orange reflection of the sun was a witness to the sunset. The prisoners in the yard started to thin out, as the guard moved on from cell to cell, counting and locking up.

He was new in this prison and followed the rules with devout respect. The counting process was finicky, scholastic, a genuine ritual. The handful of convicts who would remain outside the wards, till the second bell rang for bedtime, had to be approved by the chief warden.

"Are you a cook, man?"

"No."

"Are you a nurse?"

"No."

"Then, how can you stay out in the yard?"

The prisoners, who were taking their last hurried walk, approached the door of the 3rd ward and mutely observed the strange scene.

Here was the guard with his right hand holding his pencil in mid-air, ready to check the precise contents of the 3rd ward, with his jaw suspended, totally puzzled, wide-eyed from the paradoxical situation; and there, on the other hand, was the prisoner, who had stubbornly stopped at the door (as though striving to alter the correct number of prisoners in the 3rd ward), as though he'd been bribed to enlarge the angle of the guard's lower and upper jaw, until it was finally dislocated.

It was unthinkable! Didn't he want to go back in the 3rd ward? But Potis wasn't unreasonable. For years now, he'd been going in and out of this door, patiently, without the slightest refusal. He knew that the daily closing was only a detail of what resulted when the big door closed in a big way many years ago; he knew that nothing would change, if he remained an extra hour out in the yard, since the big door would remain closed for life.

His refusal to enter the ward had no connection with questions of liberty, society or escape. Quite simply, he was waiting for somebody, expecting someone to arrive from above, literally from the sky.

A short while ago, springtime had come. The signs were clear. First and foremost, woollen undershirts had become a nuisance; and then, the swallows had arrived, irrefutable witnesses and they'd set up housekeeping in their old nests, under the tiled rooftops. Springtime, which confuses birds as well as human beings, contrived some ash-grey tiny eggs, which soon burst open and out came molted, ugly fledglings with big mouths and breathless breasts.

The breathless breasts and enormous mouths were ascertained when the prisoners were forced to destroy nests and adopt the new-born creatures. Some huge rats, which resided permanently in the roof and all winter sauntered back and forth all night long above their heads, had recently gone in for chasing these birds, gulping down the fledglings right out of the nests closest to the wall.

This was a horrible thing for the prisoners to see. They were too sensitive to endure it. Many of them tossed about in their sleep and raved deleriously. You might answer: they shouldn't watch the spectacle. As always, they should occupy themselves with handicrafts, chess, studying, politics. But many of them spent all day and all night under these rooftops, especially the members of the Animal Lovers' Society, which just about then was hastily founded; and at the same time, most of these men were also studying in the modern biology group, a course taught occasionally to whoever had finished the basic lessons.

"Did you see that big mouth opening?"

"According to Pavlov's theory, the reflexes force the bird instinctively to open its mouth so wide."

"The same bird caught the worm again."

"According to Pavlov's theory, it's possible for the reflexes to be so strong in certain living organisms that..."

"You'll see, this one will be the first to fly."

"According to Pavlov's theory..."

So the prisoners were closely concerned about the life of the birds and when danger appeared unexpectedly, a huge stir was created in the whole yard. The birds must not be left without help. Whoever is good, but weak, must be helped. Whoever is bad, but strong, must be hindered, on all fronts. Even in our peculiar society, what is right must be our guide.

At its regular meeting, along with other topics, the members of the prison bureau discussed these nests and decided by four votes against one to destroy the dangerous nests.

With a pole they pulled down the bits of rubbish (they could hardly be called nests) above the 3rd ward, and three greedy beaks emerged and three pairs of helping hands. Potis grabbed the cleverest fledgling and could hardly find enough flies to feed it. The fly-swatter was hard at work all day long. The new nest for the fledgling was a cardboard box, equipped with more conveniences, a cotton mattress, a little glass of water, and food supplies.

Then, the training started. Its first little wings were trimmed. Pavlov's theory was applied. First of all, fasting, then flying – inside the ward, with the windows closed. After this, familiarisation; or rather, landing on top of Potis' bald head. Then right away, plenty of flies and water.

The day came when Boubouka was free to fly. A red spot on her white belly distinguished her from the other swallows. Startled, she flew up and perched on the rooftop, without moving for some time. She lacked the daring for freedom. Out there, must be the pine-trees, bushes and grass; far beyond, the sea would be sparkling; and up above, the depths of the sky, her own space.

But she remained there, staring at the prison well,

where the convicts were taking their stroll. She resembled the prisoner who suddenly received his pardon and was released from prison unexpectedly one afternoon, before he had time to familarise himself with the idea of his discharge.

Since there wasn't any boat leaving the island that afternoon, he fell asleep nearby, just next to the prison – an entire island wasn't big enough for him. The following morning, he ambled around the grey building and he kept shouting up to the high windows so the men inside would hear. This was his world and he couldn't break away. He'd lived half his life buried inside the deep well and the images from the world were blindingly bright and terrified him.

The same was true of Boubouka. Instead of flying out to the fields, she dipped and circled around near the convicts. The Animal Lovers' Society urged her to drop the sentimentality and fly away from her protector for ever. But Boubouka dove down and landed on Potis' bald head. The Pavlovian theory had triumphed.

To tell the truth, Boubouka was different from the other birds. That red spot Potis had put on her belly; her nervous, breathless way of flying – distinguished her from the free swarm of birds, which cut through the sky like swords. So she returned quickly from the yard, diving vertically and unerringly down to the target, which was always that familiar, characteristic bald head of her foster father.

He frequently spoke sweet words to her: "Where were you, dear daughter?" "Where have you been,

Boubouka?" Repeatedly, he fondled her warm gasping little belly, gently stroked her silky little wings, carried her in the palm of his hand up to his face and with his index-finger close to her beak, pretended to scold her: "Don't let those tramps, your friends, mislead you into not coming back to our den. Make sure you don't cause me such grief."

That afternoon, Boubouka seemed to have no intention of coming back. She had gone when the prison closed that noon and she still hadn't shown up. Potis was anxious as he stood there in the middle of the yard, holding his beret in one hand and peering at the sky. She was nowhere. The bell chimed extremely slowly in the dusk and for the first time, Boubouka was absent at the roll-call.

"But are you a cook, man?"

"No."

"Are you a nurse?"

"No."

"Eh, then how can you stay out in the yard?"

"I'm waiting for the bird," Potis answered entreatingly.

"What bird? I don't get you."

"My bird. The bird with the red spot. Boubouka, Mister Guard."

"Something's wrong with you, prisoner. Are we supposed to wait for your bird before closing the prison? And what if it doesn't come?"

"She'll come – without fail, she'll come."

"Our regulations don't provide for birds and such nonsense."

Potis left the door and lunged towards the back of the ward, all choked up. He collapsed on his cot and turning towards the wall, began a stifled, plaintive wail, something like a lament.

From outside, the guard shoved the iron door, bolted it, locked up, mechanically inspected the lock, absent-mindedly checked the number of prisoners in the 3rd ward on his little piece of paper, and with a nervous movement, pulled his handkerchief out of his back pocket. Removing his cap, he wiped off his shiny, sweaty bald head and moved on for the count in the 4th ward. Meanwhile, from inside, the sound of Potis' uncontrollable sobbing could be heard.

When he'd finished up with all the wards, on his way out to make his report, he was questioned by his colleague at the railing in that sector.

"Why such a delay in the 3rd ward?"

"Ah!" he answered casually. "It's about that bird, the one that flew into the chief warden's office this noon and landed on my head. The bloke's weeping. He's had a nervous breakdown."

"Has he heard the news?"

"No, he's still waiting for the bird."

Next day, when the men on fatigue-duty emptied the waste-basket in the chief warden's office, they found a dead bird. Its neck had been twisted. This gave a strange, puzzled attitude to its head; the frozen eyes seemed to be asking "why", gazing fixedly at the small, discoloured red spot on its belly.

IN FRONT OF MARX'S GRAVE

I VISITED MARX'S GRAVE. To get there, I had to walk through a park with two ponds and I saw a little squirrel to whom I offered some chocolate. He took it with his little front paws and crunched it. Then I moved on to the cemetery. In prison, I'd received a package containing some chocolate candies. Naturally, I shared them with my friends. Later on, when I had a quarrel with a certain fellow-prisoner, he tripped me up on this point: "You didn't give me a bit of chocolate!" He was a lifer, who'd lived in the mountains. Several days later, he signed a recantation and departed.

The cemetery was old and abandoned. The Jewish tombs in the back still more abandoned. His grave stands out. A big granite head. He wrote "Capital"; he loved his wife; and Friedrich supplied him with pocket-money. In the year 2000 A.D., there will be billions of adulterers. In the year 2000, at long last, "Capital" will be translated correctly into Greek (free of pseudo-popularised errors). We'll be able to enjoy Marx's verve and irony. As I munch my chocolate candy, I stare at him. Usually, people lay wreathes here or plant bombs. I keep whistling a little song "Oh Carol" (Oh Karl).

I feel like peeing. It's a secluded spot. So I slip off to one side and take a leak in a weedy patch. The squirrel pops out. (Apparently the park and the cemetery communicate.) With his front paws, he gestures to me that he's finished the piece of chocolate. "Listen, you little rat, if you're the same, I'm not going to give you any chocolate. These items must be distributed equally to all people. You shouldn't exploit having an acquaintance."

Once, I'd distributed this commodity, which is rare for prison, and I'd shared it only with my own friends. The result was that someone else recanted. It took me several nights before I could go to sleep. Because of me, one of Marx's followers was lost and now that I'm here in front of his grave, I don't want anything like this to happen to me. I sleep soundly.

Anyway, I too have recanted, of course not because they failed to give me any chocolate – there were other reasons. It was because somebody was in the habit of saying: "Vladimir used to say," and because he said it, we had to stick to it. Above all, I didn't like their calling him Vladimir, as though they were first cousins. Somebody else called him Ilitch. Karl was mentioned rarely and Friedrich even more rarely. However, they really liked uttering the phrase: "Let the Dead march on!", in the words of someone who came later. All those who came later talked nonsense.

The one I loved was Vladimir, the son of Vladimir, who had that unruly forelock and had left his imprint

"with the sledgehammer on the skull of the world"* –
maybe because he caught on early, maybe also
because of that bullet he wedged into his own skull.

It all started here with the granite head just there
in front of me: those men and the others, these men
and the men thereafter, the good ones and the bad
ones – only they got rid of the good ones fast; the
Dzugashvíli** boys barged in and exterminated them,
so only the unpalatable ones were left up at the top.
You may say to me: "Find me a pan to boil milk without spilling it." For so many years, I've been trying
just this; each morning I say I'll be careful not to let it
overflow, but I always get into the same fix. That's
how we all got into a fix, and maybe even Marx himself, because I don't think he'd want these "unpalata-
bles".

* Vladimir Mayakovsky's famous verse.
** Dzugashvíli: the real name of Stalin.

FANTASTIC!

IT WAS A FANTASTIC ERA. There were Simos' declarations (the situation critical, but not desperate); Simos was a bona fide existentialist with a beard, a shack with a soaring staircase and a donkey; these statements circulated in a special issue, alongside the politicians' declarations. It was an incredible era. The city, the people, the ideas were constantly conflicting, shifting, getting all mixed up, in a certain sense it was all a hodge-podge, and any well-organised, serious and sensible person was constantly disconcerted.

They kept digging up the streets and asphalting them. Then they installed the telephones and had to start digging and asphalting all over again. Then the same for the sewers. And the same for the gasworks. It was really a crazy era. Every day the bus terminals, the bus-stops and starting-points changed. From one moment to the next, people changed their mind. The same person who'd banged on the bus-door with his fists to get in, once he'd wormed his way inside, began quarreling with the conductor for letting other passengers get on. It was the era of the building-contractors, the gamblers, the wholesale grocers, the unlicenced drivers, the popular singers, the bouzouki-players, the demolition-gangs, the illicit love-affairs, the illegal constructions – after all, it was a crazy, incredible, fantastic era.

Externally, our hero had all the insignia of his era. The thick mug of a wholesale grocer, which often had lumps on it. Short and fat, a repulsive way of walking, a gruff and gravelly voice, a big businessman's movements. Nothing aristocratic and pedigreed about him. But internally? He had a delicate, sensual soul. He read Hamsun's "Victoria" for the tenth time and tears still came to his eyes. He was concerned about the cats whining in the cold. He found permanent refuge in adolescent themes and in the past; and he hastened there, swathing them nostalgically in dreams... There in the humble little town with the Lilliputian hills, in the provincial grammar school... In the ravine were the plane-trees, on the fence the blackberries (the fingers purple red), beyond was the twilight calm of the little meadow...

He was not of this world; he had no connection with all the motley things occurring around him. No, he didn't. So every Sunday morning, he put on his boots (given to him by a distant uncle in America) and went for a walk far away from the city, striding over the shrubs, caressing the asphodels and low pines and thinking for hours about a verse or two bars of music.

Because he was a musical man by profession. Not a cheap instrumentalist making the rounds of rural fairs, but a genuine musician from a Conservatory, with thorough studies and exercises he'd been solving for years now on the musical staves. If you started discussing music with him, you couldn't possibly escape. Double basses mingled with fugues. The tone colours fused with the low notes. *Duettino*, *prima vista* and *andante* got tangled up into a twisted ball in the course of the conversation. Anyone ignorant of musical matters, anyone whose taste went only as far as popular songs, had the impression of attending a course in Chinese. Needless to say, popular songs were out of the question. "Those unbelievable voices like Bithikotsis, those cock-a-doodle-do voices, cavernous Kazantzidis, Zambettas like doughnut batter slopping over his bouzouki, the opium-den origin, the Oriental tune was really heavy."

Other times, filled with anger, he advanced the following thought: "Whoever cashes in on the poverty of the common people, whoever offers the public decadent art (in the name of popular culture, shameful things have been done), all these bigwig bards who've fed the people dung, should be lynched by a popular tribunal some day." His classmates who'd grabbed at the fashion of *rebetiko*-music and made a fortune, he also used to lambaste with the following apophthegm:

"A good living, but a bad legacy."

And everything would have taken its course – his own consistency and mature thinking counterbalanced the contradictory, motley forces of life – he'd have left future generations his musical message and that "good legacy", and those who acted like debauched charlatans in the field of art would have disappeared in time – if it hadn't been for that spirit, which appeared at the top of the rock and stood there like a Sphinx and in her own way, asked the primordial question: "... who ends up a four-legged creature?" She appeared on that Sunday morning, when he'd put on those boots to go gadding about the mountain.

They both came to an understanding immediately; and each in his own way solved that "four-legged creature" – without any question-mark this time. He offered the philosophical interpretation, which his grey temples and paunch pressed him to follow. On the other hand, she saw it from a biological and practical angle, which had been taking shape ever since her twentieth year and the springtime embracing the entire landscape. Since a philosophical attitude presupposes thought and in a sensitive person, thought creates feelings, he fell for the poisoned bait; he wished to rely on her for ever, in order to link himself, his thoughts and his great musical message with her.

The symphonic poem springing from her body, the harmony pouring out of her legs, the warmth from her bosom would flood his notes. The percussions would express her perfect belly and hips; the wind instruments her innermost feminine being. Her classical visage would be solid form, her eyebrows two persistent rainbow-strokes audible in the background; her deep blue eyes would be an ocean of crescendoes rising upwards; and there, on her lips, the theme would be completed with a thundering finale.

However, without her being a contractor, she

understood perfectly how to make a deal with feelings. In the foreground, she played the four-legged creature with him; in other words, she solved the problem of the Sphinx in actual practice and there was a perfect balance. They exchanged "use-values" without any surplus, so neither of the two could be treated unfairly. But the ramifications of the biological complex in the field of feeling created a one-sided situation, as far as she was concerned. Would she have to become a bridge for him to communicate his own message, his own spiritual legacy, without anything in exchange? That was unfair. Before tying herself down with eternity, she wanted some kind of guarantee: A little house (where would her child stay in time to come?); a salary of five-thousand per month (my goodness, is that how people head for marriage?).

She explained her thoughts to him and he became darker than the falling night and she was colder than the rock on which they were sitting. So many unimportant people earned their living easily. Why should he insist on being penniless? In his kind of art, people earned loads of money. Why couldn't he start with the demands of fashion? He should write some *rebetiko* music, that wouldn't be the end of the world. There was time for symphonies and concertos. Later on, after making a "nest-egg" in this society, he would find his way. Life demands manoeuvering; you have to adapt yourself a bit, keep a low profile and use camouflage. Being headstrong and having a one-track mind can harm a person. And in the final analysis, do we have to do whatever we think? She'd made her decision. If he failed to act according to all this advice, they'd have to separate. He'd have to answer by tomorrow.

And she walked off, leaving him nonplussed, surrounded by the rocks; her swaying silhouette retreated until the evening swallowed her up. On his way down to the city, he felt as though he'd been looted. He found himself roaming the streets of summertime Athens, aimlessly searching for her body in the places they'd lived.

He crept into all the arcades, went up to the lofts of all the bars, entered all the remote ouzeries; searching for her tracks, he walked past their haunts, the streets and side-streets and corners they'd traversed, even once; places where they'd stopped even for a moment. A place where they'd kissed one evening and their kiss had lasted as long as the twelve slow chimes of the church clock; places where they'd parted; places where they used to meet, like that hospitable building-site where they'd made love on top of the boards one rainy evening, holding their breath in the dark, lest the passersby catch wind of them. He went everywhere – to the bus-stop and the queues waiting for the trams, which were filling up and leaving, one by one, without her body, which he'd been seeking for so many hours now.

At midnight, in a state of exhaustion, he reached his shabby room. On the little table, the familiar blank scores. Absent-mindedly, he sat down on the only chair and began writing. The babbling of a spring and a brook winding like a snake among poppies and camomile buds were covered by the uproar of cars rushing forward, just at the moment when the green traffic-lights flashed on, expelling the gentle image of the little green hills. Then her lips appeared to be growing rounder and they were transformed into red traffic-lights, forbidding any movement, any approach, any access. In the place on the paper where solitary pathways and quiet lanes were delineated, they automatically turned into noisy sidewalks overflowing with the motley crowd of people. Blinding advertisements, neon signs destroyed the depths of the sky, her eyes and the langorous white of the eyeballs remained on the paper.

He was about to accentuate her eyebrows, with those persistent curved bow-strokes, and strokes of the pick resounded in the low notes. Now a tiny *baglama*-instrument started weeping for their separation, with actual sobs. The double bass expressed the darkness of the night, while an electric bouzouki embroidered on the higher notes, forging a secret path, a pale moon emerging out of the sea. And then, a torrent broke loose beyond forms and molds, filling blank score after score. An impetuous breeze swept through the room, scattering pages of music on the floor and an infernal noise filled the room as though a pneumatic drill were at work down in the foundations.

Next morning, his classmate found him in a frantic state, collecting the pieces of paper. A huge lump had come out on his forehead; his eyes bulged; his index-finger was sticking out and as he gesticulated, he was shouting:

"The bitch will pay for this. Imagine me writing bouzouki-music! That freak is a disgrace to civilisation; I won't allow it to be heard."

And he started to tear up the music.

"Don't," his friend shouted.

The friend grabbed the scores out of his hands and began reading them. Then he sat down at the piano, enraptured, and started playing. A whole era was coming to life. With one leg in the old era and the other leg in the new. Eternal Nature was spreading out to the densely populated thoroughfares of the city. The noises of the forest mingled harmoniously with the hubbub of the city. And the whole theme was penetrated by a yearning yen.

When he stopped playing, he had a misty expression. He stood up, stared, round-eyed, and exclaimed:

"But it's incredible! It's fantastic!"

THE THIRD KIDNEY

NOW THAT I KNOW YOU CAN'T WIN PEOPLE, or even a girl, merely by words, but only with blood; now that I realise you can't possibly reach the poem only by reading, or achieve something only with camomile – forget about the people who've seen blood only on their hangnail, but still scream: "Ouch, ouch! My whole body is hemorrhaging." "You fakes, only the index-finger of your left hand is bleeding. What do you mean by your whole body?" That's why they write namby-pamby poems and masticate names with fawning admiration and endeavour to resemble certain models of theirs, without going through the fire and the inferno, which is the prerequisite of the poem. Well, it just can't be done.

Once I saw some people eating perfectly fine the night before, with the prisoners' tin bowl on their knees; but the very next morning, they had to be transferred to an insane-asylum, because all of a sudden, they felt their back was breaking and their heart was flying out of them. "My back," they kept saying, "my back"; and the tin bowl fell from their knees, leaving two drops of olive-oil, an indelible stain on the cement. It's the soul which turned black and made this break and caused this fall, despite the tenacious will of these people to go on holding that prisoners' bowl on their knees.

"Let me speak of heroes, let me speak of heroes: Mihalis." By all means, no. For quite some time now, I haven't been in this line. And I don't mean that whoever has held this huge mess-tin on his knees can reach as far as the poem. But by all means, at least one of them can. If he has given even a single hair of his testicles for this cause.

So did your mama feed you your nice fresh egg? Did you sit in the front row at school, were you a bookworm, a good boy, did you do whatever your teacher told you? Did you get pocket-money every Sunday? Did you marry a woman with a dowry and beautiful, to boot? (Some of the questions of composing a curriculum vitae before the poetasters' court-of-the-first-instance.) Come on, little boy, don't plague written texts. Poems reject you. Your words are hollow. Yes, I know, you've had a case of whooping-cough and now, you've got a cranky boss, who scolds you for even a tiny mistake. O.k. O.k. Massage yourself with alcohol and in the morning, you'll be fit as a fiddle. See here, don't keep your gas inside you, fart your problems and your worries outwards.

Now that I've charred my lungs from chain-smoking those lousy cigarettes. With the same youthful fire, I made my crescendo. Now that I've ripened together with my kidney, which has cracked open like a watermelon in the sun. Now that I've seen it (with-

out feeling any horror) opening up like a rose, no
blood or anything else, only stage-fright, and it looks
like a candied tomato. I've been stuffed with cobalt,
I'm browned off, all of me is scorched. Only now can I
reach the inferno of my mentors. Not in an external
way, by dropping the names of Rilke and Beckett, by
imitating phrases of theirs – no. Starting from my
own life, by chance I come upon my own thoughts in
their writing and this "coincidence" (so to speak)
gives me joy, but at the same time, makes me rabid.
I'm joyful because the path I've taken (the one I chose
all on my own, if you like, the path my life itself deter-
mined) is not barren, since other people (and mentors, at that) have reached the same achievement –
and that's proof, just as when you come out of a difficult exam and hurry to check up on the solutions and
everything is correct. On the other hand, I feel rabid,
because the others got there before me to record
human pain; and now, I must go still further, maybe
even by giving my other kidney.

Here I stand, plunged in thought and ready to start
an imaginary dialogue with Rilke, Beckett, Henry
Miller and other writers; obstinate, I call out to them:
"Whatever you have written in a whole book, I must
communicate in a single page, in a single phrase."
Why shouldn't I have a third kidney? Then maybe I
could transform this endless despair reached by the
mentors into some kind of hope and belief. Maybe I
could take some clay and shape a human being from
the very start and this icey firmament spinning like a
top up above us (haphazardly and aimlessly), I could

transform into a never-ending Amusement Park
assembling fireflies upon the asphalt, and making
people see the after-midnight loveliness of electricity-
poles bowing politely along the boulevards. Maybe I'd
be able to reach my first naive ideas and set up a
belief, which must dissolve as soon as the kidney is
lost.

It's not time I want – it's life I want (though the
second presupposes the first): life to squander behind
the phrases, life to build paragraphs, life to construct
a work by adding a third dimension to the word,
because the second dimension was discovered by the
others, recorded by the mentors, and I must go
beyond.

In other words, it's literally a matter of a third kidney. If it were only a problem of time, all I'd have to
do is take refuge in an artificial kidney. All they do is
to take blood from a vein and pump it into a machine.
There, they whip it up (like milk when the fat is being
removed) in order to bring it back to your artery, in a
purer form. For eight whole hours, this tune continues, two or three times per week. A machine which is
part of your body, but outside your body, prolongs
your time, giving you an extension for three, or
maybe even four years. You do gain something by
this, but what can you expend, with all these little
plastic pipes and filters; screws and nuts and electric
current?

You get some extra time, but just enough to toss
off a book full of urine, a bottle of thoughts about how
the shipwreck happened – the treacherous reef, the

desperate efforts to keep your grip on a rotten raft bereft of plans, the great overwhelming wave which is on its way. At some point, the end is close, for there's more and more urine circulating in your blood each time. "That's all there was," you say; casting one last glance at your writing, you add the title: "The Last Bottle". Stories describing veins and urine, dizzy spells, pains, stingy miseries, a business earning only what's needed to pay the accountant. Only loss, no surplus.

But I who longed to catapult phrases like fireworks, illuminating this eternal night, even for only a single moment? How can I electrify the firmament with blue and purple and red stars, without expending life? With this operation-table kidney?

I mean a poetry, which is taken *from* life, not at all costs *for* life, much more so for a purpose. So I find Mallarmé's poetry for the sake of poetry "mal-armed".* I wish that anyone, who has this yen, could have touched the prisoners' tin bowl of despair (even with his little finger) – in other words, that he could be "well-armed"* and "alarmed".* That's why, at the outset, I mentioned some mollycoddled softies (with their "nice fresh egg"), who write insipid poems; they themselves are lost in the midst of words, because they've never given a drop of their own blood for this cause. It can't be done. It just can't be done.

---

* In the original Greek text, the puns on the name of Mallarmé are left in French: "mal-armé", "alarmé", et cetera.

THE FRENCH BIDET

INSIDE US WE'D USED OURSELVES UP, without realising it. That de luxe toilet with the seahorse on the tiles as our coat-of-arms, a duck surrounded by baby ducks, swans and rainbow-coloured fish, wash-basin, toilet-bowl, bathtub, French bidet, subsidiary bidet, all of them gleaming, had played their underhanded role, termites digging away deep inside us, as worms eat wood, and now we felt hollow.

I remember when I first came to Athens from the provinces, I rented a room without any toilet. Of course there was a makeshift loo out in the courtyard, but you had to go down a pitch-dark wooden stair-case, which creaked and alarmed people. One rainy evening I got diarrhoea around midnight and I did it in a newspaper. After wrapping it up nicely (I even added a bit of ribbon with a bow), on my way to work early next morning, I deposited it in the middle of the street. Of course, you'll recall how many such packets one encountered on the streets in the old days. Some people even used to kick the packets in order to guess the contents. According to hearsay, someone took such a packet to the police without opening it and demanded a finder's reward. Oh well, once I too made a packet like this, and even now, after all these years, it makes me laugh.

In those days, I was a cheerful person with extremely few needs. I used to shave only twice a week, whenever I had a date up on the hillock with a girl, who was always in a hurry to get back home. She always acted like a truant and she had a terribly strict brother, who had the mentality of a Sicilian. So I married her. What else could I do? Rather than let them beat her up every time she returned late. Besides, this is Man's destiny, or so they say. Anyway, what with one thing and another, I found myself with all my buttons firmly in place (that's a benefit too, a kind of security). Such nicely ironed shirts for the first period, such clean sets of underwear, such polished shoes – impeccable, in a word.

She even had her own little home, a single room, but a big courtyard, and little by little, thanks to the money we saved up, we added a kitchen and other rooms too. Generally speaking, we were making progress. We acquired a fridge and a washing-machine and life became more and more convenient. Only the toilet was delaying. Out at the back of the courtyard, inside a shack, there was a Turkish hole, which forced me to crouch on my ankle-bones every morning (though it was good exercise, since I didn't usually go in for gymnastics). Inside this little shack, there was also a can with a tap, which I filled every morning to wash my hands. The regular bath was in the laundry tub. Every Saturday evening, the adventure would commence, with the wife dunking me in the wooden tub; she used to rub me so hard, she almost flayed the skin off me. Oh well, so be it.

I continued making progress. As an assistant accountant, I managed to pay off our debt for the bedroom furniture, which was really heavy, with small bedside tables and lampshades, sky-blue on my side, pink for the lady. Next, I became a regular accountant – that's when we bought our little plot of land, on the installment plan. We even planted two or three trees; at first I used to go and water them every Sunday, since my wife insisted. But they dried up, there were so many chores to be done; I was chief accountant by now, with a substantial salary, and in a few years, the house was complete – except for the toilet, which remained as the pièce de résistance, crowning twenty years' effort.

"Some day, the toilet's turn will come!" I kept telling my wife, who was always nagging me, complaining and sulking when visitors came and wanted to take a leak. Besides, we'd come so far, the toilet would be merely the finishing touch. Everything we create only once in a lifetime inspires us to make it as enthusiastically as possible; so I too did my best with this toilet, to make something truly beautiful: I added extremely expensive tiles with a strange pattern depicting various things to make me feel nice in this ambience. I also installed all the indispensable sanitary fixtures and of course, a French bidet.

I didn't mind the other fixtures. To hell with them. They were useful and anyway, at our age, it was about time we enjoyed something. Only the French bidet got on my nerves and destroyed the rest of it. That bidet. Since I'm constipated, I had to look at it for hours, and it seemed to be mocking me with its long face – its one eye was blue and its other eye red, triangular knobs on the forehead protruding just like a frog's eyes; its mouth was a drain, which sucked everything up with a sudden death-rattle when the water disappeared, and it seemed to be muttering: "See what I've reduced you to? Remember when you first arrived from the village, what a brave lad you were? You poor wretch, how did you muck up your life for the sake of a home? I'm your reward after twenty whole years of labour. So you can wash your lower parts. See where I've landed you?"

Twenty whole years of being chained to the yoke, voluntarily (that's the worst of it), in order to wind up here facing a pile of useless things – (useless, in my opinion); or even if they are useful, goddam it, they're not worth as much as this cause we call life and youth. My best years I wasted carting things here like an ant to fix up this bloody house, and in the end to construct this bidet, with its drain swallowing me down twenty whole years; and now I'm left here like a squeezed lemon, a withered face, all for the sake of a French bidet.

Despite such thoughts, I flushed the toilet and then, I went to the window to breathe a bit of fresh air and listen to the sound of the city. From all sides, a strange noise was coming. Not the familiar noise of automobiles. This was another kind of noise – a persistent splashing sound drowning out any other din. The entire basin of Attica had been transformed into an immense bidet and we were all of us sitting on top of it, washing, washing, washing ourselves, while hundreds of thousands of toilet-tanks poured down whole waterfalls, hailing our Progress.

"SKOPEFTIRION":
HEROES' SHRINE FOR SALE

THEY SAY THAT THE BLOOD POURING out of the van was covered with carnations by some true patriot's hand. After a few years, there'll be legends about flowers sprouting out of the asphalt, these same flowers which maybe once someone had indeed left there on top of the dark stains. Maybe old women will even tell their grandchildren, like a fairy-tale, that on certain evenings in May, the street used to look like a meadow full of poppies.

Mythification and hyperbole. In truth, the blood was left to dry up in a few spots, till the rain washed it away – and only on the asphalt, because inside the main gate, the blood was absorbed by the dirt path and became one with the dust, leaving no traces behind.

Nowadays, nothing exists to remind us of the executions. Only a few smudges on the corners of Skopeftirion Street, supposed to cover the letters which the other side had written in red paint during the first months of the Liberation: "National Sanctuary Road"; everything has faded, blue smudges and letters underneath, both red and blue are gradually dis-

appearing, a new discoloured hue is barely dis-
cernible, produced by mixing these two colours, only a
hint of what happened, of what was supposed to happen, of what finally did not happen. On one hand, the
attempt to allow a few marks to exist; on the other
hand, the tenacious will to have them wiped out for
ever, so that the place would not remind anyone of
anything – in the course of time, brought about this
hybrid chromatic smudge, a common street without
any face, without any particular history, like so many
streets in Kesariani, like thousands of streets in
Athens.

Nevertheless, from those events, there are secret
marks which cannot be distorted, which escape the
obsessive effort of certain people to conceal and bury
everything deep down; there are hidden marks which
the experienced eye can discover. There are the birds
which fly out of the grove in alarm, darting upwards
in a swarm as though startled by secret volleys of
gunshots. There are the cypress-trees which cannot
keep their fruit; the blood is transfused from the roots
to the shoots and the cypress-cones fall off. There is
all that underground blood.

And furthermore, there's the wind swirling rubbishy bits of paper, letters from another era which
have turned yellow, paper from a cigarette: "I'm leaving with my eyes turned towards..." (the rest is
washed out); a worn-out cap with an address on the
threadbare lining; a torn piece of underwear, full of
dried up sperm: "my darling wife", scribbled with a
black pencil dipped in saliva; and other small scraps

of paper – "my son", "my brothers", "comrades".

Skopeftirion Road and all these things together are still there and get entangled in the feet of any unsuspecting passerby, who tries to kick them away; they pursue him till he turns the corner and disappears. Afterwards, the dustman passes by with his little cart: "Why did they send me here? The street is spick-and-span." The street is indeed clean. The whirlwind has lifted the rubbishy bits of paper high up, very high up above the rooftops. But the moment will return for them to fall at the feet of the passerby and he'll curse the mayor for not sending somebody to collect the rubbish; they'll come back again, because some day messages *must* arrive, even if they're delayed thirty or forty years, even if they're old and forgotten, even if the people to whom they are addressed are dead, these messages must be sent, because who can endure the grievance:

"I was executed; I wasted away in a mass grave; they threw lime in and buried other people on top of me; I turned to greasey earth; I became only memory, until it too faded gradually, as my mother's life faded out; but some day, you must pick up that scrap of paper I threw on the street; don't let it drift astray. Justice."

The district council is in session. Topic: How to cherish the dead, memorial services, funeral sweets and priests. Some of the councillors suggest a modest ceremony with an archimandrite (but not a bishop too); the others who take a firm stand on sacred bones, draw their swords and demand a bishop at all costs, a grandiose church ritual, a dedication of wreathes in the area where the executions had taken place, a master of ceremonies, assistants and other organisers to arrange the programme, dances, declamations, songs, all the pomp.

Of course, the majority is guaranteed and the decision has already been made in the "inner circle"; the general directives have been issued from "down below"; everything's arranged by the Party: who will do the weeping and when, which tone of voice they'll use and precisely what they will say. The council session is being held as a sheer formality; no speech can possibly change the programme; no proposal will be granted, however wise it may be. Despite all this, there are some councillors who ask leave to speak and there are others who suspect they have no official role on the actual day of the festivity, so they're in a hurry to say something right now "concerning the Dead", in order to show off a bit to the few persons listening to the district council.

I receive a note from a certain colleague, who more or less shares my viewpoints. "How long is this claptrap going to last?" I want to answer him on the same piece of paper: "What's to be done about this exploitation of the dead every year?" I wind up twisting the note into a tiny airplane and all the while the claptrap continues, with those heart-rending high notes – "our hallowed Dead" – every so often, I feel tempted to sling it at the bald head of any speaker at all, Left, Right, it makes no difference, they all provide the same target sitting there in a circle around the table.

The chairman gives somebody further down leave to speak, so that the same gramophone words can be heard again, always the same opinions, and frequently with the very same movements, and the speech is always garnished with the phrase "our hallowed Dead". That word "our" puts me in a devilish mood; how can certain people claim the dead as their own private property? I ask leave to speak:

"Mr. Mayor, colleagues, surely you must be aware that among the Greeks executed in the Skopeftirion Grove, there were also some 'van-vaulters'. I request that we see to dedicating a wreathe to their memory." Needless to say, they ordered me to stop speaking; I tried to carry on, but they made me shut my mouth; others reviled me; somebody in the audience shouted: "You desecrator".

I have in mind those hardy lads whose counsellor was hunger and who instead of an ideal, aimed at winning an extra tyre. They arrived in front of the ditch absolutely alone, without any hope that their party would hold a memorial service for them, without any kind of vindication afterwards. How can one offer moral support for their loneliness? The others had people to weep for them, hundreds of wreathes, slogans, songs and poems. The others, most of them, had something to fall back on, a vision, a cause they believed was making progress, regardless of whether this too was ruined in the end, there were those who continued and would some day reach their great goal; and at that point, at the rallies, their offspring would proclaim the names of those who had fallen. On what ideas could a van-vaulter fall back?

"I jumped onto the van and ripped open the hood with my knife. The other people were running behind, waiting for me to toss them the stolen goods. Then I saw the Germans sitting in there with guns. Anyway, I'd have jumped down, but I thought I might endanger the others. So I let them catch me. I thought it would be like the time before: Averoff Prison, a small tree, which nips off some years. But they sent me to Haidari. And now I tread the beaten path inside the walled camp up to the trench; and the only thing I can think of is not to step on the grass, which is still standing upright. I did no great deeds in my life; I never thought about ideas and such things; at least, for these last moments, don't let me harm even the grass."

The Secretary of the Shooting Club received us. I don't remember his name, but I can pick him out among a thousand other persons: thin, rather short, and with grey hair. He met us where the target dummies are, at the thirty metre firing range. He spluttered: "Which memorial service?" and he kept gesticulating; his thin throat was ready to burst, especially at the moment he said: "In other words, if the roof of your house collapses and kills a dozen people, their relatives will be entitled to hold a memorial service every year in your home?" His throat was just right for strangling; as he was uttering these words, you could stick your thumb there and start squeezing,

squeezing away till his voice ceased coming out of his windpipe. Or you could put him in the pen there, along with the dummies, in that thirty metre firing range. "Get lost, you skunk," you could shout at him and take aim somewhere under his legs; go on shooting, let the bullets tintinabulate all over those dummies: "Dance away, never fear, I'll allow your relatives to hold a memorial service for you every year, even though it's an accident – where can I find a roof out here in this open space?"

You'll see, in the end they'll chop it up into plots of land – six metres by twelve, exactly enough to get legal permission. As far as land is concerned, they'll all agree, Right, Left, and Centre; despite any other differences, their common denominator will be that "little plot".

For a start, the "Refugee Association" will put in a bid for it, regardless of which block the management belongs to. Then the "Labour Association" will join in the fun, in order to provide shelter for the workers. After this, the State will join in to hand out the keys. Of course, some sort of school will be built, but without a schoolyard; and the children's recess will be out on the road.

I don't know if in the end, the little grove will be saved. The correct thing would be to wipe it out too, so there won't be any leeway for busts or any possibility of a Heroes' Shrine, cenotaphs, candles.

Naturally, the area up beyond the graveyard won't be chopped up into plots of land. On the contrary, they'll decorate it and go on continuously improving it. As a matter of fact, recently they erected a large cement cross to remind us of the "big pit". But when you search for it, you can't find even a little pit, not even a pothole. At any rate, gradually this area will earn its new name from the frequent memorial services and the schools visiting it to dedicate wreathes and future visitors will reflect that perhaps somewhere nearby, there had once been a "big pit" full of chauvinists' corpses.

It's probable the name "Skopeftirion" – Shooting-Range – will remain, but neutral, without any specific meaning, in the style of Syndagma – Constitution Square; it will remind people of the idlers who used to shoot at cardboard targets, at little plates made of clay and at pigeons. At human beings, never. At the time of the German Occupation? But did anything like that ever happen?

CONTENTS

MARIOS HAKKAS

Hakkas was born in 1931 in the town of Makrokomi, in the province of Phthiotis. In 1935, his family moved to the working-class, refugee neighbourhood of Kesariani, where he grew up and lived most of his tragically brief life. After completing regular high school, he studied at the Pandeion School of Political Science between 1952 and 1954. But his studies were interrupted, when he was arrested for his political beliefs and put in prison for the following four years, most of the time in the prison for political idealists on the island of Aegina. In 1959, he was drafted into the Greek Army, but as a muleteer. His experiences for two years in the army and the preceding four years in prison gave him abundant material for his first collection of short stories, entitled "The Enemy's Rifleman", published in 1966. A small collection of poems, entitled "Beautiful Summer", appeared about the same time, as well as several plays for the theatre. In 1967, after the Colonels' coup, he was arrested again (though not for long this time) and in 1970, his second collection of short stories, entitled "The Bidet", was published by "Kedros". As of 1969, he was the victim of cancer, which – after three whole years of brave resistance and intensive writing – finally killed him on July 5th, 1972, just a very few days before publication of his third and last collection of short stories, entitled "The Brotherhood" (or perhaps better, "The Communal Cell").

AMY MIMS

With a B.A. in ancient Greek Literature and History from Harvard and another degree in Byzantine and Modern Greek from Oxford, Amy Mims has made her permanent home in Greece since the 1960's. She has translated two of Kazantzakis' travel books and almost 400 pages of his letters to Eleni Kazantzaki contained in her *Biography*. She has also translated various works of Ritsos and her five creative books include her prose-poem *Eleven Seastones for Yannis Ritsos*. Between 1980 and 1990 she translated approximately 20 plays by modern Greek playwrights and for the past many years has been working on the English translation of Ritsos' largely autobiographical book entitled *Iconostasis of the Anonymous Saints* and her own autobiography covering these past four decades in Greece, entitled *The Minotaur and 2* (33 years in the neo-Greek Labyrinth).

KOSTAS MOURSELAS *Red Dyed Hair*
Novel. Translated by Fred A. Reed

ARISTOTELIS NIKOLAIDIS *Vanishing-point*
Novel. Translated by John Leatham

ALEXIS PANSELINOS *Betsy Lost*
Novel. Translated by Caroline Harbouri

NIKOS-GABRIEL PENTZIKIS *Mother Salonika*
Translated by Leo Marshall

SPYROS PLASKOVITIS *The Façade Lady of Corfu*
Novel. Translated by Amy Mims

VANGELIS RAPTOPOULOS *The Cicadas*
Novel. Translated by Fred A. Reed

YANNIS RITSOS *Iconostasis of Anonymous Saints*
Novel (?) Translated by Amy Mims

ARIS SFAKIANAKIS *The Emptiness Beyond*
Novel. Translated by Caroline Harbouri

DIDO SOTIRIOU *Farewell Anatolia*
Novel. Translated by Fred A. Reed

STRATIS TSIRKAS *Drifting Cities*
A Trilogy. Translated by Kay Cicellis

ALKI ZEI *Achilles' fiancée*
Novel. Translated by Gail Holst-Warhaft